MAGIC LILLY

and the Vampire with the Wiggly Tooth

By KNISTER

illustrations by Raimund Frey

Translated by Kathryn Bishop

minedition

This is Lilly. She
has a book. It is not
an everyday book.
It is a book of magic.
One day it just
mysteriously appeared
beside her bed.
Just like that.

There are all kinds of magic in this
book. There are silly spells and crazy
tricks.

But beware…

Don't say the words out loud. Oh no.
For there's no predicting how it could go.

For if the words aren't exactly right,
the next cookie you try to bite,
might become a sour pickle
or salty fish on pumpernickel.
Your toothbrush might become a broom
with an ugly witch
flying around your room.
Your teacher might

become a frog
or a quacking duck
or barking dog.

Lilly hasn't told anyone about the
book. She is a secret
magician.

Lilly has a little brother
named Leon. He really
gets on her nerves
sometimes, but she
loves him anyway.

Leon Is Bitten by a Peanut

There was no school today. Lilly and Leon were at home, but their mother had to work. So Lilly had to make breakfast for Leon.

"Fix me some breakfast," said Leon.

"What do you want?" asked Lilly.

"I want a roll with lots of peanut butter," said Leon. "And I want it with extra peanuts, too!"

"That's not breakfast," said Lilly.

"Mama let's me!" said Leon.

"Oh, okay," said Lilly. "But just a few extra peanuts."

She fixed the roll and gave it to Leon.

"Here you are, you big baby!" said Lilly.

Leon was hungry. He took a monster-sized bite.

"Ouch!" he yelled.

"What's the matter now?" said Lilly.

Leon dropped the roll.
He put both his hands up to his mouth.
  "The roll bit me!" he said. "Or maybe
it was a peanut. I'm bleeding!"
  "Oh, don't be silly," said Lilly.
  But Leon was bleeding.
  "Let me look at it," said Lilly.
  She looked in his mouth.
  "It's your tooth!" she said.
  Very carefully, she wiggled it with
her finger.
  "Leon, it's your first loose tooth.
When it falls out, you'll be big."
  But Leon was not happy.

"I want to be big now," said Leon. "And I want to put it under my pillow for the tooth fairy. Pull it out right now. Please!"

"No," said Lilly. "I'm afraid. What if I hurt you? You have to do it yourself."

Leon tried. He couldn't do it either.

Lilly tried to make Leon feel better.

"You wait," said Lilly. "It will fall out all by itself."

Leon cried, "But I can't eat! What if I can never eat again? What if I die? No. The wiggly tooth has to come out. It has to come out now."

"Oh hoppin' hiccups," said Lilly. "What should we do?"

The Dentist Fell on His Behind

"Mama can pull it out. I'm sure," said Leon.

"I don't think so," said Lilly. "When I had a wiggly tooth, she took me to the dentist. He pulled it out with one quick pull."

"Did it hurt?" Leon asked.

"It didn't hurt me," said Lilly. "But it did hurt the dentist."

She was making up the story a little bit now.

"He pulled so hard, he fell...right on his behind. I lost my tooth," she said.

"But the dentist broke a vase and a lamp, two glasses and a stool, some pliers, two drills, and even the waste paper basket."

"I don't think I want to go to the dentist after all," said Leon, looking a bit nervous. "Besides, I need to eat. I can't wait for the dentist."

Lilly felt sorry for Leon.

"You could eat chocolate pudding or vanilla pudding or banana pudding! What about rice pudding?" said Lilly, trying to make her brother feel better.

Then she made a very funny face. "You know, it's different with vampires," she said.

Leon looked at her.
"How is it different?" he said.

"Because," she said, "when a little vampire loses one of his special teeth, he gets very, very hungry. You know which ones I mean — the sharp, pointy teeth. The ones that are good for biting."

"The poor little vampires," said Leon. "I'll bet they get really hungry!"

Leon wasn't thinking about his own tooth anymore. So Lilly told more of her story.

An Exciting Vampire Story

As Lilly told the story, Leon listened very carefully.

Victor Vampire will never forget. It was his fifth birthday. Because it was his birthday, he got to stay up late.

At midnight, he was going to go around the castle. He wanted to scare a few people. He wanted to bite a few people. But it was not yet midnight, so Victor had to wait a little while.

There was no TV back in those days.
So he sat and watched a big spider
weave its web. The spider had just
caught its dinner.

That made Victor think about eating.
"I'm hungry," he said.

So his mother made him a
treat that all vampires love. It was
a sandwich of crusty black bread
and...blood sausage, of course.

Then it happened. He took one big
bite and OUCH! His tooth...it was
loose and wiggly.

He ran crying to his mom. Suddenly, her spooky vampire face looked even spookier.

"We have to pull your tooth," she said. "That way a new tooth can grow. There is no time to lose. If we don't hurry, you are going to get very hungry!"

And as quick as a bat, she started to pull. She pulled and pushed.

She wiggled it left and right. She wiggled it back and forth.

But nothing happened! The tooth just wouldn't come out.

"We have to wake your father," said Victor's mother. "He'll be able to fix it."

She walked over to the coffin where Victor's father was sleeping. She knocked on the top. Nothing. She knocked again. Still nothing. There was only a wheezing, rattling sound. Victor's father slept a deep vampire sleep until…

...the clock in the old tower struck twelve.

"Who is waking me so soon after midnight?"

It was a deep, scary voice. It sounded close, but somehow far away. Then there was a loud CREEEAAAAAK! The lid started to open. Little by little... finger by finger...you could see a wrinkled old hand. It was gray—the color of an old rat's tail.

Victor's father was awake. He slowly climbed out of his coffin. A vampire's face can frighten anyone, but when he saw his wife and son, he smiled and simply said, "So my dears, what can I do for you?"

His voice was like thunder! It was so spooky that two flies fell off the wall—scared to death!

"Our Victor has a loose tooth," said his mother.

The old vampire tried to wiggle Victor's tooth, but he couldn't pull it out. His vampire fingernails were too long.

"There's only one thing to do," said Victor's father. "You have to bite your tooth out."

"Bite my tooth out?" asked Victor.

"Yes. Just take a bite of my coffin. That should do the trick."

Victor made a funny face.

"Your great-great-great-grandfather did the same thing," said the old vampire.

Victor was not very happy. As a matter of fact, he didn't like the idea at all.

His mother said, "Can I have a bite too? It has the wonderful taste of blood chocolate!"

"Blood chocolate," said Victor. "Wow!"

And he took a big bite. Both of Victor's special vampire teeth were now in the lid of the coffin. His parents laughed. Their voices were so loud and spooky that a whole group of flies fell off the wall—all scared to death.

Even Victor started to laugh. The coffin didn't taste like blood chocolate. It tasted more like an old shoe, but the trick had worked. His teeth were gone.

And Victor's new teeth? Well, if you looked very closely, the shiny tips were already beginning to show.

A Haunted Castle in the Bedroom

"That was good story," said Leon. "If we had a coffin, I could take a bite."

"Try biting the chair," said Lilly. "I'll bet it tastes like chocolate."

Leon laughed. "I'm not falling for that old trick. But we could play vampire."

Lilly thought it was a good idea.

"Go in your room and get a blanket," she said. "You can wear it like a vampire's cape."

Leon flew to his room. That was what Lilly was waiting for.

Lilly quickly got the secret magic book that was hidden under her bed. She was sure she could find a trick that was just right for playing vampires. Something that would make it more fun.

Sure enough on page 2398, Lilly found what she was looking for: *Vampire Magic*.

Lilly was a bit unsure. She hoped the trick wasn't dangerous.

Lilly heard Leon calling from his room.

"I found a blanket," he said. "I look like a REAL vampire."

"You wait," thought Lilly. "I'll show you who has the best vampire tricks!"

She said the magic words and *VAVOOSH!* In an instant, Lilly's room looked completely different.

There was no more bed, just a pile of straw. There was no more closet, just an old wooden chest. There was no lamp, just a big candle holder instead. The walls and floor were made of stone.

Lilly was speechless. She couldn't say a word. She heard her little brother. He sounded so far away. When she opened her door, she couldn't believe what she saw. The whole apartment had turned into a haunted castle, just like magic.

A Little Vampire Wakes Up

Leon was standing in the hall. At least where the hall used to be.

"What's going on?" he asked.

Lilly didn't know what to say. She pretended everything was normal.

"Well, you said you wanted to play vampire."

She took Leon's hand.

They went into the living room. At least what used to be the living room. Now it was a great hall. The Hall of Knights. And there was a big table in the middle. There were even fancy rugs hanging on the walls.

The TV wasn't there anymore. Instead there was a big spider web. And in the corner...Lilly couldn't believe her eyes. In the corner stood a real coffin!

Suddenly Leon saw it too. He held Lilly's hand even tighter.

CREEEEAAAAK!

The lid started to open. They knew what that meant! But they couldn't move. It was as if they were frozen. They just stared at the coffin.

A little vampire climbed out. He was the same size as Leon. He had real vampire teeth and wore a black cape. He also had gloves as white as snow.

"Victor?" asked Lilly.

"How did you know my name?"

"Just a guess," she said, but she was beginning to worry.

The little vampire's voice was so creepy, it gave Lilly goose bumps. Leon held her hand even tighter now. He was afraid.

"You wouldn't mind, would you," asked Victor, "if I had a little bite? I haven't had breakfast yet."

His vampire teeth sparkled as he ran toward them.

Lilly was fast. She jumped to one side and pulled Leon with her. She knocked down one of the knight's chairs and a vase and kept running.

They had to hurry. They had to keep going. They ran to the table, and Lilly pushed it over.

She had seen that in a movie, but it didn't help. The little vampire just ran around it.

"I only want a snack," said Victor. "What wrong with that?"

Lilly could tell that Victor was enjoying chasing them.

Lilly ran out of the living room and pulled Leon with her. She needed her magic book, but it was in her bedroom.

"Oh, hoppin' hiccups," said Lilly. "That vampire's fast."

Victor ran ahead of them and blocked the door.

The Strike of the Vampire's Tooth

Lilly thought for a moment. They had to get out of the apartment. She would worry about the vampire later. But the vampire tripped Leon, and he fell down hard on the stone floor.

"I smell blood," shouted Victor as he leaned over Leon.

Leon was afraid and put his hands over his face. Lilly ran into a dark gloomy room and she reached into a trunk where the refrigerator had been. She yelled, "You dumb vampire, go ahead...bite my brother. But just don't bite my blood chocolate."

Victor the vampire stopped instantly.

"Blood chocolate?"

Victor shot into the kitchen. He saw
Lilly. She had something in her hand,
and like lightning, he took a big bite.
POOF!!

Lilly was suddenly standing in the kitchen. In her left hand was a bundle of garlic. In her right hand was a white glove.

Leon came running into the kitchen. He had his wiggly tooth in his hand. It had fallen out when he fell down.

There was no vampire. He was gone. There was only the white glove, and the apartment had returned to normal.

The Trick with the Garlic

Leon was so surprised. He could only stutter. "But...I...where...how did you..."

"Garlic," said Lilly. "Vampire's are afraid of it."

"If they bite garlic, they disappear. I knew Mama had some in the refrigerator. I just reached in and grabbed it."

Leon didn't know what to think. He was confused. He didn't really understand and didn't know what to say.

At that moment, their mother came home. Leon ran to her. But she had already seen the mess in the house.

Lilly and Leon's mother was not very happy. She didn't let Leon say a word.

"What has been going on?" she said. "The table is turned over, a chair is on the floor, and my pretty vase is broken. Was there a herd of wild horses in here?"

Leon opened his hand. In it was his wiggly tooth.

She saw the gap in Leon's smile —
the gap where the wiggly tooth had
been. Leon looked so cute, she couldn't
stay angry.

"The wiggly tooth, Mama," said Leon. "First I was sad but Lilly ...and the vampire also had...he was here! Lilly saw him too. And Lilly said when you lose your first wiggly tooth...well... then you are big."

Their mother smiled at Lilly and said, "That's so nice of you. Not all sisters play so nicely with their little brothers!"

"Hoppin' hiccups! That was close," thought Lilly, and she smiled and hid the white glove behind her back.

"Well," she said. "We always find something to do—just like magic!"